W9-BIM-489

A ROOKIE READER

PURPLE IS PART OF A RAINBOW

By Carolyn Kowalczyk

Illustrations by Gene Sharp

Prepared under the direction of Robert Hillerich, Ph.D.

CHILDREN'S PRESS
A Division of Grolier Publishing
Sherman Turnpike
Danbury, Connecticut 06816

Library of Congress Cataloging in Publication Data

Kowalczyk, Carolyn.
    Purple is part of a rainbow.

    (A Rookie Reader)
    Summary: Introduces vocabulary and the concept of
parts of a whole with examples such as a petal on a
flower and a whisker on a kitty.
    1. Readers (Primary) [1. Vocabulary] I. Title. II. Series.
PE1119.K77   1985   428.6   85-11693
ISBN 0-516-02068-4

A petal is part of a flower.

A raindrop is part of a shower.

6

A feather is part of a bird.

A letter is part of a word.

A finger is part of a hand.

A drummer is part of a band.

A smile is part of a clown.

A jewel is part of a crown.

A tire is part of a truck.

A bill is part of a duck.

18

A building is part of a city.

A whisker is part of a kitty.

A sail is part of a boat.

A beard is part of a goat.

24

A window is part of a house.

A tail is part of a mouse.

A child is part of a family.

And a family is part of this
big, big, big, big WORLD!

WORD LIST

a	family	purple
and	feather	rainbow
band	finger	raindrop
beard	flower	sail
big	goat	shower
bill	hand	smile
bird	house	tail
boat	is	tire
building	jewel	this
child	kitty	truck
city	letter	whisker
clown	mouse	window
crown	of	word
drummer	part	world
duck	petal	

About the Author

Carolyn Kowalczyk loves writing and children. She has a degree in Psychology from the University of Oregon and is inspired to write by her experiences in foreign countries. She studied in France, taught English in Japan, and is presently in Germany writing and working as a nanny. Through books we learn about the world, and when we learn more about the world we see how very much the same people are. Especially children!

About the Artist

Gene Sharp has illustrated several books in the Rookie Reader series including *Too Many Balloons* and *Please, Wind?* He would like to dedicate the pictures in this book to Laura who loves pictures and Alan who is learning to also love the words.